MY FIRST GHOST

By **MAGGIE MILLER & MICHAEL LEVITON**

Illustrated by
STEPHANIE BUSCEMA

Disney • HYPERION BOOKS
NEW YORK

To all our wonderful ghosts—M.M. & M.L.
For my grandma and mom—S.B.

Text copyright © 2012 by Margaret Miller and Michael Leviton
Illustrations copyright © 2012 by Stephanie Buscema

Printed in Singapore
First Edition
1 3 5 7 9 10 8 6 4 2
F850-6835-5-12105

Library of Congress Cataloging-in-Publication Data

Miller, Margaret, 1979–
    My first ghost / illustrated by Stephanie Buscema ; [text by] Margaret Miller
& Michael Leviton. — 1st ed.
        p. cm.
    Summary: Provides the reader with a ghost of his or her own, as well as
instructions for feeding, caring for, and playing with this spectral friend.
    ISBN 978-1-4231-1949-4
    [1. Ghosts—Fiction.] I. Leviton, Michael. II. Buscema, Stephanie, ill. III.
Title.
    PZ7.M628My 2012
    [E]—dc23   2011017596

Reinforced binding

Visit www.disneyhyperionbooks.com

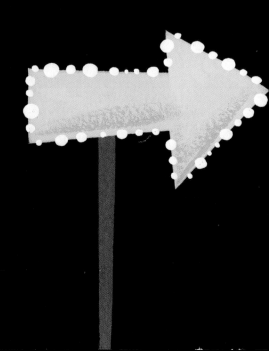

This book comes with a free ghost inside.
Your ghost is between the next two pages.

FREE

Ghost!

INSIDE

Turn
Page

WARNING:

A ghost is a big responsibility.
Are you sure you want a ghost friend
of your very own? If not,
CLOSE THIS BOOK NOW.

To claim your free
ghost, just turn
the page.

CONGRATULATIONS!

Your house is now officially haunted.

Your ghost is probably standing next to you right now, reading over your shoulder.

Of course, you can't see, hear, or feel your ghost.
Ghosts are invisible and silent.
They take up no space at all.

Your ghost might be a little nervous
about meeting a new friend.
Your ghost might even be scared of you!

Ghosts are often afraid of:

Kids

Parents

The Dark

Monsters

Ghosts

So please smile at your ghost.

Don't make any faces that might scare your ghost.

A ghost is like a pet, but better.

Your ghost will never chew your slippers.

Your ghost will never steal your breakfast.

Your ghost will never wake you up
by sitting on your head.

A ghost is like a brother or sister, but better.

Your ghost will never
hog the bathroom.

Your ghost will never
punch your arm.

Your ghost will never
sing annoying songs
for hours on end.

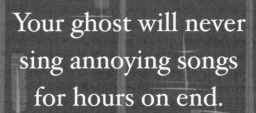

Ghosts do not eat or drink.

Please do not try to feed your ghost.
But pull up an extra seat at the table so your ghost
can spend lunchtime with the family.

Ghosts don't get dirty.

Please do not try to wash your ghost.

Be sure to keep your ghost healthy.

Please perform regular checkups.
Use your thermometer. Your ghost should be
exactly room temperature.

And be sure your ghost
gets plenty of exercise.

There are many ghost-friendly indoor activities.

Play hide-
and-go-seek.

Paint a picture of
your ghost.

Invite another ghost
over to your house.

Or, take your ghost outside to play.
Ghosts are very good at tag.

Ghosts are very bad at catch.

Life with a ghost isn't always easy.

Your invisible,
silent friend
can be hard to
understand.

But if you know what to look for,
you can tell when something's not right.

If you're talking to your ghost and you hear a noise behind you,
it means you should turn around—you're facing the wrong way.

If you shiver even though it's not cold,
it means you bumped into your ghost.

If you sneeze three times in a row,
it means you've forgotten your ghost is there.

You can also tell when your ghost is happy.

When you giggle even though nothing is funny,
it means your ghost just told you a joke.

When you get the hiccups, it
means your ghost is tickling you.

When you yawn, it means your ghost is hugging you.

Do you **love** your new ghost friend?

If you love your ghost,
your ghost will haunt you
forever.